THE

DARKNESS

A Bulwark Anthology

VOLUME 8

BRITTNEY LEIGH

This is a work of fiction. Names, characters, places, and
events are either the product of the author's
imagination or used in a fictitious manner. Any
resemblance to actual persons, living or dead, locals or
actual events is purely coincidental.
This work is an anthology of Bulwark.

DEDICATION

To Franklyn,
Together we found the light at the end of the
tunnel.

CONTENTS

1

Dear Diary,

To anybody else, you would think a town like Bulwark is just plain boring. It's a small community, quiet, more like a village than a town. Our whole population is football crazy. The high school is the focal point of our home, and that makes football the center of our attention.

Prep rallies and homecoming events are our Oscars. The towns people all come out to cheer our native sons and daughters, making them feel like royalty.

Behind the facade of this folksy atmosphere, I'm afraid to admit there is something more, something darker. Most people say not to take it too seriously. After all, every town has its secrets.

That sounds okay to most people, but then again, I'm not most people. Mom always

told me, *Sophia Beachwood, curiosity killed the cat.*
I have only one thing to say to that.
Meow.

2

Dear Diary,

Guess who is now the head reporter of the Bulwark Bugal? You're looking at her! Or rather, you are reading her words. Chloe, my bff since the 5th grade was made a photographer, so it's a match made in heaven.

Next weekend we'll be covering Bulwark's Fall Leaves Festival. TMI? Perhaps you're thinking "Nerd Alert" - well, all I have to say to that is it keeps us busy.

The Fall Leaves Festival is an exciting time of year. The basic bitch in every girl comes out with her Uggs on and a pumpkin spice latte in hand. Couples walk hand in hand picking apples, and kids roll around in the field gathering pumpkins. There's a potato sack game that leads the day, followed by an all you can eat apple pie eating challenge, and finally we end the festivities with a tug of war, topped by the Homecoming Football game.

Now, to be honest, I've always felt that the tug of war is the only one that matters. Every year, without fail, the winner of the tug of war is crowned the Fall Festival champions of the year. I've always thought it was rigged. Maybe this year I'll finally find out and get to write about it in the school paper. At the very least, I'm gonna stick next to Chloe like glue. She has an appointment with Christopher Caltrese for a photo shoot. He's… well… the best looking guy in school and she's taking pictures of him in his football uniform. You know how a girl likes a man in uniform. I'm tagging along to drool.

3

Dear Diary,

OMG! I can't believe this. Something magical is happening. Christopher Caltrese, spoke to me! Yes, that's right, ME! Now, I know, you're probably thinking, "Sophia… don't get your hopes up…,"

I didn't think he noticed me, not when I went with Chloe for the photo shoot. I didn't think he'd give me one thought.

What can I say about Christopher Caltrese? Only that he's the most gorgeous hunk. Wait a minute, I am forgetting that I'm an ace reporter. Let's keep this professional. Christopher is head of the football team. You would think that's a perfect match as I am a cheerleader, but I'm not head cheerleader. That title belongs to Grace Kelly. Yeah, you heard me, her parents actually named her Grace Kelly, who was some queen or something in France or Italy, I think. Yeah, and her daughter ran away to join Cirque de Sole or, maybe she ended up on a reality show.

Well, any who, Christopher is soooo good looking, with his long, sun-kissed hair and chiseled abs. He's got these amazing shoulders and... did I mention he's like the smartest kid in school, too?

I haven't had much luck with guys. You know on those TV shows where the parents tell their daughter, "Boys only want one thing"? Well, I learned that the hard way.

All these stupid boys are finally discovering what their dicks can do, and they want to test it on every girl they can swoon over. Either way, it sucks for the girl. If she says no, she's a tease and if she gives in, she's a slut. So much pressure. Damned if you do and damned if you don't. The parents are no help, I mean... you know what they are going to say. Girlfriends are in that middle ground; it's all about who you talk to.

It's sad, really. All I want is that fairytale ending. HEA, happily ever after, if you're like Chloe and don't ascribe to that sort of thing. That Prince Charming guy who cares about me and actually wants a long term relationship. I'm sure you're shaking your head and thinking "Prince Charming doesn't exist." Yeah, yeah... I know... but why not? Why not reach for the stars and try to get as close to them as you can? If Prince Charming doesn't exist, then why not try with the most popular guy in school at least… right? I mean, he's gotta be someone's Prince Charming, why not me?

My friend Chloe insists I'm pretty. She says I am the Meghan Markle of Bulwark. I don't know. Two eyes, snub nose, wide mouth. I guess having mixed race parentage helps make me look more exotic than cute, but that smattering of freckles just ruins everything, IMO. Chloe keeps telling me they are adorable, but I think she's much prettier with her long dark hair and gray eyes.

I may not be the brightest kid in the class, but I'm not stupid by any degree. My grades are always way above average, and while I'll never be a Rhodes Scholar, I know I will make Georgia State, no problem. The one thing I know I can do, is write. I mean, I am school reporter, duh!

A little more about Christopher. He's like, 6 feet tall, built with muscles, star quarterback for Bulwark High's football team, and bonus, he's Italian! Which means he knows about that good Italian food! Blonde and Italian, go figure. Chloe says it's probably Crusader heritage.

His parents are wealthy, New York money. His father, Louis Caltrese, used to be the head editor-in-chief for a popular fashion magazine. Christopher was already in demand because of his financial status and all of the cool stories he had. He's been hanging out with the glitterati his whole life. Bulwark must be a real bore for him.

His father only moved to Bulwark because he felt he had made enough money. He was ready to get out of the city atmosphere to relax with his wife and kids. Christopher's mom, Mary Caltrese, is your typical stay-at-home mom.

One time she came to the high school during a late night football practice and brought her homemade sausage and peppers dish! She brought enough for the whole team and the cheerleading squad. All my mom ever brought were those annoying doughnut holes.

So you must be wondering why Christopher finally noticed me. I'm glad he never saw me stalking him in the hallways. Well, we happen to be in the same English class and his last test grade wasn't so hot. He shared to me that Mr. Davis, our teacher, had to make a call to his parents about getting his grades back up.

Everything sort of fell into place. While I've struggled with other subjects, English Lit was not one of them. It's my one straight A class. Christopher, however, is not doing as well.

Today when Mr. Davis let us out of class and everyone was gone, Christopher came up to me. He seemed embarrassed and awkward about it, too. He hemmed and hawed, like some shy guy, which we all know he is not! I'm sure he didn't want to admit to his shortcomings. Christopher asked me to walk with him. So, I gulped and said okay while trying to stop from hyperventilating. While we strolled through the halls, which had unfortunately emptied by now, so no one was witnessing this fall festival miracle, he confided in me! He told me that Mr. Riley, the football coach, would sideline him for the homecoming game if he didn't get his grades up on the next test.

That's a big deal. Huge deal! Our star quarterback not playing during homecoming would be like Tom Brady not playing during the Super Bowl. It would severely hurt our whole team. He asked if I would help him with the next chapter of The Great Gatsby.

Would I help him get through the next chapter of The Great Gatsby? You bet. Jay Gatsby and Daisy Buchanan, here we come!

Wait till I call Chloe! She is just gonna die!

How I am going to concentrate on the troubles of the idle rich of Long Island while looking at Christopher, I don't know? Well, wish me luck!

4

Dear Diary,

While everything is getting rosy on the personal level, I'm starting to feel like a slave to the Bulwark Bugle. They're not approving any of my work, at least not without editing the crap out of it. Plus, I'm trying to pull at the emotions of my fellow students and write about what they care about, find the truth and expose it. Pulling emotion from this generation is like getting gum out of your hair, complicated and a pain in the ass.

I felt by writing heart wrenching stories it would motivate students to take more interest in the world around them. There are a million things that need to be addressed, like the fact that police are profiling minorities, equality, women's rights. I know I come off as an airhead, but I know the difference between right and wrong. More than that, we need to talk about what's happening on a small scale, like in the school. I recently wrote an article on the effects of AstroTurf on school grounds. The school board replaced the football fields grass with artificial turf over the summer. Ever since then, the field hasn't been the same. I felt it was my duty to inform my fellow students that our beloved football field had been covered with infection causing chemicals due to the fake grass. When I questioned the school board I was instead told, "If you want to write about the football field, Sophia, you can write about the homecoming events and future sports game played on that field." I was starting to think I'd never get a real news article published.

I write amazing pieces, if I may say so myself, yet the truth get lost once the chairman of the paper starts editing my stories. See… I try to write important stuff, not just about Thelma Green's awesome apple relish. To be fair, I understand my readership is more towards a bunch of high school kids. I know my stories weren't going to be Pulitzer Prize winning articles, but I felt like everything I wrote was being censored. I have the distinct impression that my articles are being censored

I even got turned down at the Fall Leaves Festival when I started asking questions. I guess this town isn't as welcoming as I thought. Ever since Billy Joe Parker, the janitor's nephew went missing the town has been on curfew. My reporters nose is indicating that something's rotten in Bulwark, I smell a cover up...

5

Dear Diary,

This one is strictly for your eyes only, okay? Last night I had a sleepover with Chloe, you know, the usually. We ordered pizza, baked cookies, and watched a movie. Tonight's movie was Cruel Intentions. After the movie, Chloe and I like to discuss the characters and what we thought about the plot, but tonight was different.

"You know that scene when the girl was teaching the other one how to kiss?" Chloe asked me, quietly.

"Yeah… " I replied, not know where she was going with this.

"Do you ever think you'd kiss a girl?"

"Well, I guess, yeah, it's not my thing, though. I expect to see more of that, like in the movies we watch. It always happens at a random college party or something." I answered. I never really had given much thought to it. I mean, I was boy-crazy. Always have been. Chloe knew that. I turned away for a moment to get another cookie from the plate resting on the side table. When I turned back, Chloe grabbed the back of my head, leaned in and kissed me!

"Woah, um, what was that?" I was stunned. I didn't know what to do. Did that just happen?

"I'm sorry, I shouldn't have done that." Chloe said. She was clearly embarrassed.

"It's okay, Chlo. We're best friends and nothing's ever going to change that, okay?... But why did you do that?"

"Well, I… I've never kissed anyone before. I've never really had feelings for someone like that. After watching that movie, I felt like, like you're the only one who I've ever felt anything for. I don't know what that means, but I wanted to give it a try."

"Aw, Chlo… you know I love you, but in a best friend kind of way. Right?" I really didn't want to hurt her feelings, but I wasn't going to let her stand in the way of my chances with Christopher.

"I know, me too. I'm sorry. I let the movie and my feelings get the best of me."

We hugged, it wasn't awkward like you might think. It was comfortable.

"Chlo, I want you to know this changes nothing. I will be here for you no matter what. I want you to be whoever you want to be, and kiss whomever you want to kiss. Okay?" I said looking Chloe in the eyes.

Chloe nodded, her face serious.

"Pinky-Promise," I replied with a wink. We linked our pinky fingers together in solidarity and turned in for the night. I stayed up for about an hour thinking about the kiss. Was Chloe in love with me? I'm sure it was just experimentation. It is high school, after all. We're all trying to discover ourselves here.

6

Dear Diary

I did it! Not that, you lurid thing. I'm keeping this PG for now. I just had my first tutoring session with Christopher. We met at the pizza place and he had a slice and pop on the table for me when I walked in. Talk about Prince Charming.

He insisted we eat first and you know what happened? Everything faded away and it was magical. I didn't see or hear anything for that hour and a half we sat together. The jukebox played, I heard it when I walked in, but for the life of me, I can't recall a single song.

We never even cracked a book. We talked and talked. I can't even remember what we spoke about, but Chris has this low voice, and I had to lean close to hear him speak. I could feel his breath feather against my cheek, and let me tell you, it sent chills down my spine.

He talked about how hard it has been for him! Really? Star quarterback, most popular kid in school is having insecurities?

Several times, I placed my hand on his forearm and patted it, letting him know how much I sympathize with his plight. I mean, come on, handsome and sensitive. This is the Prince Charming jackpot. This guy is the Holy Grail of men. He is freakin' perfect.

He has these soulful blue eyes that look like they hold everything inside. I kept staring his large square hands, wanting to lace my fingers within his. But I held back. This was supposed to be a study group and I think we were specializing in studying each other.

Well, we barely opened a book, when I looked at him and asked, "Chris, you're so smart. What's going on?"

He sucked in a deep breath and looked around the room as if he wanted to confess his deepest secret to me. The door opened and Sheriff Finnes walked in, tipping his hat at the man behind the counter. The sheriff paused looked around the room and his gaze rested on Christopher and me. I saw Christopher stiffen, and turn his face away.

Well, like I told you before, dear diary, my curiosity is sometimes my biggest flaw, I squeezed his hand. He looked up and said, "Come on. Let's get out of here."

THE DARKNESS

We grabbed our books. Ever the gentleman, Christopher threw out our trash and we rushed out the door. I looked behind to see Sherriff Finnes clench his hands into fists.

Oh, phones ringing… it's Chloe. I gotta go. I'll finish this later.

… I'm back! Let me tell you what happened because the afternoon ended way different than I expected.

What happened was so amazing, so fantastical, so… scary, that I had to process it before I put pen to paper.

Christopher and I walked away from town. I have to describe Bulwark, Georgia for you. There is a small town center with a diner, library, sheriff's office, and a movie theater. There's also some small stores, an auto repair, and a pharmacy. We've got a hospital, funeral home, and of course there is the high school with a ginormous football field. Most of this town is surrounded by rough brush, gullies, and farms.

People have lived here for hundreds of years. I think the town was settled in the late 1600s by Pilgrims, or something. I know there was a massacre and a lot of the settlers were murdered. They say there were survivors, but none were ever found. When the ships returned the following year from Europe, all they found were the smoldering fires of the crude huts. However, every few generations, Mr. Frakes, my history teacher says, a blue-eyed native pops up. He is writing a paper for some history journal and has shared that he thinks they were assimilated into the local tribes. Speaking as a mixture of various people, I don't see anything new with that.

But, that's not what this entry is about, anyway. Back to Bulwark. The Civil War had a vicious battle here, and again homes were destroyed and all sorts of terrible things happened. I can't say I have much sympathy for the Confederates and am thankful one side of my ancestors were liberated. I shudder to think where I'd be today if the South won.

We walked away from civilization, such as it is in Bulwark along the rutted roads leading to Old Jericho, the main road of the county. Occasionally, Christopher pulled me along, a frisson of heat going down my arm where our fingers touched.

Soon I was breathless, not sure if it was from carrying my books or loping after Chris who seemed to walk faster the further we got from town. I must admit, the way he kept glancing over his shoulder gave me a fine case of the creeps, yet I couldn't stop following him even if I wanted to.

Finally, I dug my heels into the dirt and said, "Not a step more, Christopher. I want to know what's going on in your head."

19

Christopher wiped the gleam of sweat from his forehead. He was perspiring. I placed my hand on his overheated cheek and said, "Whatever it is, you can tell me."

"It's hot out here."

"It's Bulwark, Georgia," I said with a smile. "Let's go sit under that tree."

Chris nodded and taking my hand in his, dragged me toward the tree. I had to wipe the grin off my face. I couldn't help the feeling of belonging with him, as though his possession of my hand felt like we were more than just friends.

We settled on the hard ground, he pulled up a blade of grass, shredding it. He pulled another and I took it from him. "I'll teach you a trick."

He leaned back against the tree, but I could tell he was still tense and nervous.

"When I was a little girl, my dad taught me how to do this. If I ever got lost, all I had to do was call." I placed the blade of grass between my lips and blew. It gave a mournful wail that echoed in the dense brush.

All around us, it grew quiet, all the rustling stopped. Chris did the strangest thing, right then. He leaned forward, cupping my face kissing me gently on the lips. Well, let me tell you, I felt the thrill of that kiss all the way to my toes and had to stop myself from leaping into his arms.

"You make me feel safe," he said, his voice low.

WTF? I wanted to shout. Trust me, some of my mom's southern manners took control and I just sat back with a shocked look on my face. "What?" I said instead.

"This place. I... it's strange. I don't feel safe."

"Bulwark is the safest place in America," I retorted. "I would be scared in your big cities up north."

Christopher shivered as if he were chilled. I leaned forward taking his hand within mine. "Tell me."

He looked around, as if to confirm we were alone. "It's my locker."

OMG, you could have knocked me over with a feather. His locker? His locker! I didn't know how to answer. My mother's voice filled my head with her admonition of being careful what you wish for, but I smothered those thoughts when I looked at his shamed face. Whatever was troubling Christopher, it was as real as the trees around us.

I moved closer to him, placed my arm around his shoulder and said, "I have no idea what you are talking about, but I'm here to listen."

Christopher sighed as if a large weight had been taken off his back. "You know it's not easy being me."

I laughed then. "Yeah. I feel real sorry for you."

"No." He smiled. "Being popular, leading the team, keeping my grades… you know keeping everyone happy, it's a lot of pressure. It's like I'm constantly on. Back in New York, I was average, barely noticed…"

This was news to me. I figured he was as popular there as he was here.

"Here… I have to keep to maintain this standard… like I'm perfect or something."

I nodded, and thought he was doing a rather good job at it.

"Well, I think the stress finally got to me."

"What makes you say that?"

"I told you. It's my locker. First it was the smell."

"That's usually easy to explain. Old clothes, a forgotten sandwich…" I started, but the look he gave me froze the words in my throat.

"I keep a clean locker, Sophia. It was a smell like I never experienced before. It was dank… horrible." His voice lowered to the merest whisper. "It was evil."

"Whoa. evil, like how can a smell be evil?"

Christopher shook his head. "I can't understand, only that I just knew it was something dark. Very dark."

I sat back wondering how I was going to question him. He looked pale as a ghost, and his hands a bit shaky. He didn't resemble my strong quarterback, at all.

I kind of understood what he was saying about pressure though. It's hard to maintain friends. Harder to keep the weight off. Grades were constantly fluctuating. Life was filled with landmines. I guess I could understand the position of trying to stay on top of a mountain. It's a slippery slope and filled with all kinds of potholes everywhere. Christopher's voice interrupted my roiling thoughts.

"And you know what else. I think Billy Joe is in there."

"Billy Joe Parker?" I blurted. "Nah. I heard he ran away to Tennessee to escape that crazy family of his."

It was getting dark. I could hear the bullfrogs start to croak, the mosquitoes buzz around our heads. I slapped a few of those suckers away. We needed to get home. Christopher's eyes gleamed with unshed tears. This was starting to freak me out.

"No, I think I heard him calling from inside my locker."

"Have you told Scott about this?"

Scott was Christopher's best friend. They were always together. Christopher stayed silent, but shook his head.

"No."

"Oh Christopher, you have to tell somebody."

Christopher nodded and shrugged. "I'm telling you."

Inside his locker? Most girls would have run for the hills, but then I have to remind you, dear Diary, I am not most girls. Remember the cat comment? Aside from that, I am a reporter and this was getting more and more freaker by the minute.

"I think I may be going crazy," were the next words from his mouth. I had a sudden vision of my Grandma Bella who is half Cherokee, whisper in my ear, you sure you want to continue with this guy?

I squashed the thought of her, and bit my bottom lip. How to go on? Christopher, the perfection of the entire male species was telling me his most intimate vulnerabilities. He was smelling and hearing things, at least he wasn't seeing things.

"Not only that," he continued. "I see a fog seeping out of those vents in the locker door."

Well, there goes that. Still, I stared at his beautiful face, thinking even perfect is still nice, if it's mildly flawed. After all, he was coming to me and that alone made it interesting. It proved we had a special trust between us.

Who could I even confide in? I thought. If word of this gets out, his fear of being toppled from his position on the pedestal was in jeopardy. No, it was up to me to help him through this.

I stood up and brushed dried leaves from my jeans. Christopher stood, shaking off his jacket and swung it around my shoulders. My heart picked up a fast staccato that felt as though it would burst from my chest. I flooded with sympathy. I had to help him.

The growl of an engine made us both spin. Sheriff Finnes patrol car blocked the narrow road. He got out and dramatically held up a flashlight in the fading light of day.

"What are you kids doing out here," he demanded.

I moved closer to Christopher and felt him tremble. "Nothing," he replied sullenly.

"I thought I told you to stay away from this area." Sheriff Fines walked toward us, making me feel like I wanted to back away. He seemed furious.

"There's nothing near here but that old abandoned mill, Sheriff. It's Bulwark. We're perfectly safe."

"Nobody's safe anymore, anywhere, Sophia. Don't let me call your parents and let them know I found you out here alone. I'm guessing your dad wouldn't be too pleased with you."

I swallowed and said, "I'm not alone. I'm with Christopher."

If the Sheriff's eyes were lasers, I bet I'd be dead on the spot. He shook his head and said, "Skaddle, you two. Now!"

We turned and stumbled at bit, but I fought the urge to turn around and look. Curiously overcame me, though, and I did. The Sheriff's steady gaze was directed towards the bushes camouflaging of the old mill. For some reason his expression worried me. He turned and when we made eye contact, I realized he was not just concerned, he was angry.

The reporter in me resurfaced and I decided I needed to get to the bottom of Christopher's mystery before I could even consider tackling the sheriff's warning."Let's go over this one thing at a time. When did it start?"

He placed his strong arm around my back and we walked down the long road home.

"Just after Billy Joe disappeared. One day I noticed that stench. I cleared out everything my locker. I mean… everything. I came up with nothing. I stopped leaving stuff in there."

"The odor. Did it transfer to your things? Like a jacket or uniform? Did you ask anyone if their locker smelled?"

Christopher scrunched his brow.

"No, I stood by a few of the other guys spots and never smelled it anywhere.

None of the odor transferred to my belongings. And, something else… I was the only one who smelled it.

"Hmmm… interesting. Maybe it was sewage moving up from underground, isolated to your locker."

Christopher shook his head. He stopped dead in his tracks and made me look up at him. "It's not sewage. You don't think I'm crazy?"

I shook my head. "I believe you."

Christopher sighed then and it made me stop to really look at him. I realized something. I wasn't thinking about how cute or smart he was. The giddiness that filled me before when I thought of him was replaced by a peaceful calm. I took his hand. "I really believe you. We'll figure this out."

7

Dear Diary,

The internet is a wonderful thing and I set right away to figure out what was going on. I googled Bulwark, odor, disappearing teens and was rewarded with a rich array of responses. It seems Bulwark had been a hotbed of dark deeds for years. Our own sheriff was involved in some child stealing issue with a supposed witch only last year over by the area behind the old mill. There were rumors that a house appeared and some crazy woman was stealing children. It was rumored that the sheriff's own child had been abducted. But then, his kid was home again, there was some bad accident where a lot of people died, including the deputy and the whole story was squashed. All I could find was more town gossip and hinds, nothing solid.

28

I also had a faint memory of some gooey substance that flooded Old Jericho Road, but that had vanished by the spring and when we brought it up in school, it was quickly dismissed.

I picked up my cell to call Chloe. I had enough of keeping this to myself. I needed help.

"Hey Chlo, How are you?"

"I'm stuck on the constitution assignment, like I really give a crap. Did you finish yours yet? Can you share your notes with me?"

I was quiet, I wasn't even listening to her.

"Sophia? Are you there?"

"Yeah… um, I have something really weird to share with you… but you have to promise you won't say anything."

"Sophia, you know you don't even have to say that with me. Did you finally do it with Christopher?"

"Do it? No.. no, I have something to tell you…" I didn't know where to begin.

"Chloe, Christopher thinks there's something strange going on in his locker. He says there's a dark fog that comes out of it. It smells really bad, and he can hear that kid, Billy Joe Parker's voice talking deep inside."

There was dead silence for a minute and then Chloe said in a whisper, "My locker smells too…"

"What?"

I nearly dropped my phone, "Why didn't you tell me?"

I must admit, I was a little shocked, especially after Chloe shared her thoughts on her sexually. I thought we were always on the same page, as if we read one another's minds.

She replied, "I was waiting until I was really sure before I said something. I took my mother's disinfectant wipes and sanitized every locker on that hallway."

"When did you find the time to do that?" I was aghast.

"I gave the janitor, you know, Trout Parker, fifty bucks to open all the lockers and clean them with me."

"Ugh, I hate that guy. I hate the way he looks at us. He's such a creep."

"I had no choice, Soph."

"Well, did it get rid of the smell?"

"No, it's still there… I don't know what to do."

I chewed on my fingernails for a bit, not quite sure how to proceed. I was scrolling down Google when a web link caught my eye.

"Sophia, are you even listening to me?" Chloe began to sound frustrated.

"Wait a minute, I think I found something."

I opened the link and there was an old newspaper clipping with the headline, "Local

Tribe Protesting Bulwark High School Being
Built On Sacred Indian Ground"

"Wow, you're not going to believe
this!" I read the article aloud to Chloe.

"1908, Mayor Helman authorizes the
construction crew to begin building the newly
planned Bulwark Secondary School despite it
being on an Indian Cemetery."

"I don't believe it! I feel like I'm stuck
in a Steven King movie!" Chloe said.

"I know," I replied. I thought for a
minute and added, "Chloe, what if we take a
picture of the inside of your locker? Maybe
we'll find some clues… I'm gonna speak to
Christopher tomorrow morning after class.
We need a plan. We have to do this together."

8

Dear Diary,

After math class, I hung back in the hallway. It felt like I waited forever. For some reason, Christopher was taking a long time speaking to Grace Kelly. Maybe he was getting a some notes he missed, but I didn't see any papers being exchanged. It was clear to me that Christopher was troubled. He probably needed to discuss football business with her. Still, I tried not to let the resentment I felt filling me spill out. He likes me, I know he does.

I wondered if I should go in and tap his shoulder, but something kept me in the hallway. To my relief, he looked my way and smiled that special grin and whatever I was feeling disappeared. It was like all of my worries melted away.

"I told Scott," he announced as he walked toward me. He definitely looked more at ease with the whole situation. I guess I must have persuaded him to open up. I believe sometimes people need a push in the right direction.

"Great," I responded. "I told Chloe."

He frowned at this and I asked, "What?"

"I didn't want to share this with the whole school." Christopher accused.

"I'm sorry. I just felt like we could really use the help." I felt my cheeks color up with embarrassment. Christopher must have been upset because he didn't seem to care that he was making me uncomfortable.

"Chloe. Really. That's your idea of a good defensive."

My throat grew tight, and I felt tears smart my eyes. Where was the sensitive guy I sat with a few days ago? I didn't recognize this Christopher. And then he kissed my cheek.

"I'm sure you did what you thought was best," he said, his face looking contrite. "What's the plan?"

I didn't have a plan yet, but I was sure we should start with Chloe and the pictures.

"Let's meet back here at six tonight, after practice. We'll each take a picture of the inside of your locker."

"With our phones? Can't we do that right now?" he asked.

"Let's do it when there are no distraction in the the hallways."

Christopher agreed. He nodded his head and muttered, "Makes sense."

"Chris, what's up with you and the sheriff?" I asked.

Christopher scowled, "I used to hang out over by the old mill."

"Why? That place was condemned. It's not safe" I must have made a face, because Christopher looked annoyed.

"It's what we did, okay. Billy Joe and I. We took Billy Joe's dogs for a walk and… we smoked some weed there, okay. Billy was having a great time training the dogs to do some tricks while we shared a joint. The sheriff found us getting high and let us go, but he was pretty pissed. You'd think he never smoked weed, or something." He became thoughtful. "I think… I think, he was more mad at us being there than anything else."

"You do that a lot?" I asked feeling a shade of disappointment. I'm not really into that kind of thing myself.

I saw Scott shift his feet and move away. HIs lips were compressed into a fine line.

"Nah. Occasionally," Christopher said with a shrug. I caught Scott shake his head from the corner of my eye.

The bell rang and we scattered to our next class. I turned around to watch him leave and I called, "See you at six."

9

Dear Diary,

I couldn't wait to fill you in on all the news. OMG. We saw something. I can't believe it. There really is something strange and horrible happening in the school.

We all met at six. The school was pretty much empty by then. We could hear the cleaning staff moving desks as they mopped the floors down by the music rooms. The tile floor was tacky with cleaning solution, and the halls smelled like disinfectant.

Chloe was nervous. I could tell because she couldn't stand still. It looked like she had to pee really bad. Scott was leaning casually against the end locker, his face grim. He seemed so serious. I never noticed Scott much, he was always in Christopher's shadow. Scott is shorter, and much thinner than

Christopher. His brown curls often fall over his hazel eyes. He's not on the football team, but he responsible for the scoreboard. I think he has bad asthma or something. I realized he was staring at me. I don't think we had ever had a conversation. I said hello to him and was surprised when his face turned beet red. He looked away from me then.

I shrugged and began, "This has to stay between the four of us. We're not even supposed to be here right now."

Christopher shook his head and said, "No shit. I can't risk my reputation."

I paused for a minute, and tried to read his face. The lighting was dim, and for some reason I couldn't figure out why he seemed so hostile.

"Well, I've been doing some research," I said, whipping out a folder. I opened it and showed them the information I found the night before. Chloe raised her phone and took a quick snapshot of the article. All three of us looked at her.

"What? It's for research." Chloe said. I couldn't help but to laugh. That's just how Chloe is, unpredictable. Christopher grabbed the folder. He studied it, taking in any information he could find.

"You found all this?" Christopher examined. I nodded.

"You're a regular Lois Lane." Christopher joked.

"Does that make you Superman?" Scott asked.

I shifted feeling a bit on edge. I wanted to like the fact he thought I was being a reporter, but somehow his comment made it feel snarky. I opened my mouth to say something, but Christopher's head was down and he was totally absorbed in the article. "It's saying, this school was built on a native American cemetery?"

Chloe pointed to a paragraph over Christopher's broad shoulder.

She read. "Look here, the article says back in the 1600s, Native Americans believed that this land was spiritual. They would pray to the water gods because where there is water, there is life and food to hunt. When they reached this land they discovered a large green puddle that would continue to replenish itself even during long droughts."

Scott looked up at me. "Do you think that's what's been smelling up their lockers? Maybe this puddle is back, resurging through the school?"

Christopher replied, "Dude, what about the voice I heard?"

"An echo from the other side of the locker?" Scott asked.

Christopher's back stiffened, and his brows lowered. "You don't believe me?"

"I believe you," Scott replied. "I'm just saying it's… well… you know. A voice in your locker." He shrugged.

Christopher was looking madder by the moment. I placed a hand on his shoulder and said, "Relax. Anybody would question something like that."

I don't know, but he looked with that same angry expression at me. I felt Scott move closer to my side.

"I'm telling you, it sounded like Billy Joe. I'm certain of it. I couldn't make out what the voice was saying, it was muffled…" Christopher looked over at his locker. He took a big swallow and said, "I haven't told anyone this yet, but last night, I had a dream. Billy Joe was in it. At first he was running through the football field with his dogs, he seemed happy. But then it went black and all I could hear was yelling, but it didn't just sound like him, there were others… "

I didn't even know that Christopher was that friendly with Billy Joe Parker. I thought Scott was his best friend. But I wasn't getting that vibe right now. Instead I told him, "It's okay, Chris. We're going to figure this out. Okay, let's do this…" I flung open the smelly, old locker. The stench was overwhelming. A misty fog slithered out onto the floor. We all backed away. I sent a look of apology to Christopher, but his eyes were glued to the gloomy cloud sliding out of his locker.

Side note: I'm seriously surprised the school hasn't done anything about this yet.

Chloe reached for her phone, took a picture and froze. We didn't see anything, but Chloe did. Her face bleached of all color and I could swear she wobbled as if her legs couldn't hold her up.

"Chlo, are you okay? What do you see?" I was staring at her frightened face.

"You were right… It's Billy Joe… look…" Chloe stammered.

"Woah… what the…? How is this even possible? Christopher, can you still hear him? Try talking to him or something," Scott shouted.

For Scott and myself, this was the first time we actually experienced what Chloe and Christopher were talking about. I looked at Scott with my eyes wide. "I can't believe this!" Nobody was listening.

"No, I can't hear him. So far that only happens when I'm alone," Christopher replied.

The lights flickered and the locker door slammed closed as if pulled shut by an unseen force. A howling wind enveloped us, chilling me to the bone. Lockers started opening and closing, the noise deafening. My knees went weak and we huddled together. Someone grabbed my arm dragging me toward the exit. I was surprised to see it was Scott, not Christopher, who was way ahead of us. As we were running, that old janitor, Trout Parker, raced into the hallway, yelling, "You damn kids, what are you up to now?"

All four of us screamed.

"Come on, follow me." Christopher yelled. He ran toward the back of the school and we all stumbled after him. Scott still held my arm. I saw he had Chloe by the hand, too.

Christopher was ahead of us, by at least a yard. He flung open the doors and we found ourselves racing toward the football field.

The smell of the locker surfaced again, but much stronger this time. As our sneakers hit the AstroTurf it felt squishy and wet. I sunk into the muck, my shoes filling with liquid.

That gross puddle I read about seemed to appear and it was saturating the football field. The smell was overwhelming. There was a group of people standing in a circle in the middle of the grass. Their faces were covered with bizarre painted masks that resembled no animals I ever recognized. They were covered by long gray blankets. They were chanting *bind them, free us* over and over again.

We stopped short banging into each other. We stood in the shadows of the bleachers where the darkness cloaked us.

"Who are they?" Scott whispered.

Chloe fumbled with her phone to take pictures.

Christopher gulped then replied, "I don't know and I don't care. Let's get the hell out of here."

I turned to leave then stopped abruptly. "Wait a minute. This is my school. I want some answers. Hey... Hey!"

"Stop, Sophia." Chris grabbed my arm, but I shook him off. I was mad.

"I see you! Who are you?" I yelled to get their attention.

Chloe stayed back, frozen with fear.

I turned to see Scott and Christopher walking behind me, I continued to march over to them, when lights surrounded them, we heard a loud pop and they were... gone.

"What just happened?" I heard Scott ask. "Where did they go?"

"We scared them off." Christopher said with no small amount of pride. "Hey, Sophia, maybe if you do your grass trick we can find them. Scott, check this out." He picked up a blade of AstroTurf grass and blew on it. The synthetic grass made a screeching howl.

"See, this fake grass does the same thing."

"It's not meant to find other people. I already told you, it's a call to make if you're lost."

42

I wanted to say, *and who scared them off*, but kept my tongue firmly in my mouth. I was getting a little annoyed with Christopher, when Scott seemed to be on the same page as me.

"Who scared them off? Tiny little Sophie, that's who, you big dork."

Christopher bunched his hands into fists and it looked like he was going to attack Scott. I raced between the two of them and put my hands up. "It doesn't matter right now. We have to find out what is going on in Bulwark."

"That was creepy. Who do you think they were?" Chloe walked toward us.

The two guys were still staring at each other like bulls in heat. There was some dynamic I didn't quite understand here. I thought they were best friends.

"I think your trick is cool, Sophia." Scott said to me. I smiled at him, and looked down. Something else distracted me.

A paper lay abandoned on the grass. I walked over to pick it up. It was a page that looked like it had been ripped out of a book. It was filled with strange symbols and writing that looked like a spell of some sort. I held it up.

"by the grass in the fields
by the water it yields
our grounds we protect as our shield

to see thee and free thee"

"What do you think it means?" Chloe asked.

I shook my head. "Not sure, but either way it can't be good."

"So the question is, do we tell the parents?" Scott said what I was thinking.

Christopher responded. "No way. Nobody is going to believe us."

"I'm going to research this paper. One thing's for sure, this will be going in the school newspaper!" This was a real story! A real mystery. I mean, what the heck was going on in this school? I'm glad I was in the thick of this.

"Sophia! No! Don't even think about publishing this. If not for me, you wouldn't even know about it, remember? I can't take that risk. I have a reputation to uphold." Christopher said.

"I understand," I replied, feeling uneasy. "How could we not say anything? We have a responsibility to our fellow students. Our friends." I couldn't believe Christopher was only worried about what people would think of him. I was disappointed he wanted to keep this a secret after everything we just saw. This was on school property. "Don't the students, staff members, and parents have a right to know what's going on here?"

Scott nodded. "Lives may be in danger."

"My story. I say when we let others know. If it turns out to be nothing we are going to look really stupid," Christopher retorted.

I responded, "Chris… did you see what just happened? That was *not* nothing." I realized I was speaking to air. Christopher had walked away.

Dearest diary, what did I ever see in this guy? I just found out why Christopher has been failing his classes. He's been getting high with Grace Kelly after school. How did I find out? Well, after cheerleading practice I saw Christopher go over to Grace Kelly again. I heard Christopher say "Tonight, at seven? Okay, I'll be there." As my mom would say, *curiosity killed the cat*, and I was more curious than ever. So I decided to do a little spying of my own on Grace Kelly. I wanted to see what she and Christopher had been up to, so I planned a stake-out with Chloe. We headed to the grocery store and loaded up on snacks, because what's a stake-out without snacks. After the store we headed to Grace Kelly's place. At first, it was boring. Chloe and I just sat around eating our Cheetos.

"Is there a point to this? I'm starting to get antsy." Chloe said. Her knees were perched up on the dash of my car.

"Be patient. I know something is going down tonight. I overheard Grace Kelly and Christopher talking. Something is happening tonight, I know it. Of course Christopher's late. He said seven and it's already 7:45 at night..." I said. I was positive I knew what I heard.

"Pushing it a little close to curfew, Sophia… our parents are going to start bugging out if they see we're not home in time," Chloe said anxiously.

"Curfew starts at nine. We have time. I'll make sure we're fine," I responded. I didn't want to give up just yet. I was going to find out curfew or not.

Right then, I saw Christopher pull up in his white mustang. Grace Kelly came running out of her house, opened Christopher's car door and jumped in. Well, Diary, they lit up a blunt and we're laughing the whole time. And then, they kissed! That's right! I thought Christopher was all about me, but I guess not. I can't believe Christopher is into this. Extremely disappointed, I started my car and sped off.

"Woah, you didn't want to spy more?" Chloe said.

"I've seen enough. It's over. I'll still help him with his locker situation, but that's it."

I was furious. I really thought Christopher and I were end game. I have no time for romance right now. I have a mystery to solve.

10

Dear Diary,

Christopher called me later that night as if nothing had happened. Well, of course nothing *had happened* as far as he was concerned. For me, it was a whole other can of worms.

Christopher and I had a huge blow-out fight. I brought up the Grace Kelly situation.

"Why? I wanna know why." I was furious with Christopher.

"What? Sophia, what are you talking about?" Christopher was clueless. I was beginning to think Christopher was a little dense.

"You gave me clear signs. I can maybe get over the whole pot smoking thing, but then you kissed Grace Kelly? Of all people, Grace Kelly? Why?" I was ready to let him have it. The southern belle gloves were coming off. No more Miss Nice girl.

"Sophia… what? Wow, you thought just because I was nice to you that we would run off into the sunset together?" Christopher replied. How rude! I can't believe I was so easily brushed off.

"After everything we've been through? You know, I thought you were different. I thought you weren't like the other guys… but it turns out, you're worse. You tell girls what they want to hear, make them feel close to you, you kiss them and act like it means nothing…" I was about to continue but Christopher interrupted me.

"Sophia, I thought you were smart. I needed help with my grades. I didn't know you would develop feelings for me. Well, maybe I did. But then, I can hardly blame you."

I felt myself tense, I had to fight the urge to throw my phone at the wall. I don't know why I stayed on the cell listening to him. Maybe it was the thrill of the new story. I had to admit, I was feeling a little sick to my stomach about the whole thing. Christopher went on, oblivious to my growing disgust.

"It doesn't hurt that you have access to the school newspaper, either. So, yeah, I opened up to you… that doesn't mean I want to *be with you*. You're a nice girl. Listen, I gotta go." Christopher said, followed by a click on the phone. He hung up. That was it.

What an ass. What a piece of… you know what. I'm going to hold back. Oh God, there's my mother's southern charm kicking in again.

11

Dear Diary,

Scott called me out of the blue and asked if we could research some things together. After my conversation with Christopher, I have to admit, I was weary. It seems he filled up a whole notebook with observations and interesting theories. At first I talked about meeting up, but then I realized Scott was committed to our cause. We arranged to meet up at the school library to do some more research after class. I had all sorts of questions, how could he actually be friends with a total dick like Christopher? At this point, I wasn't in the mood to be charitable to Christopher or any of his friends. While Scott seemed like a nice enough guy, I was definitely feeling gun shy.

My Lois Lane gene was kicking in, though, and there was some investigating that needed to be addressed. Like, who were those people on the football field last night? What were they doing? What does the strange piece of paper with that weird message left behind mean? We went straight to the computers to find out.

"Scott, I have an idea... give me a sec..." I had the password to all of the schools archived news articles, and today, we were about to put it to good use.

"Here we go. Don't tell anyone I just did that," I said to Scott.

He smiled and asked, "Where'd you get the passwords?"

I don't know how much I trusted this guy right now. After all, he was buds with the douche, Christopher. Still, I have a certain amount of pride in my connections and replied, "Oh, you know, the perks of being the school's resident nerd."

"Oh come on. You're too pretty to be a nerd."

I stiffened like a startled cat. Narrowing my eyes, I looked at him to see if he was ribbing me. Scott stared back, face relaxed. He was fiddling with the computer mouse and seemed innocent enough. I just didn't trust him right now.

"Your secret's safe with me." He winked at me and I felt my resolve melt a bit.

I cleared my throat and began explaining, "Well, we know this school was built on sacred native American land…" I typed in a few search words to get us started.

"Hey, look at that, it says here the tribe buried here was a Cherokee tribe." Scott pointed out.

"Omg! This is perfect. My grandma Belle is half Cherokee. She may have the answers we need, Scott!" Finally, I felt like we were getting closer to solving this mystery. *Why didn't I think of this before?* There was always whispers of Grandma Belle's ancestors being involved with all sorts of weird stuff within the Cherokee heritage… but I'm not sure. She never opened up to me about that. She probably felt I was too young to be exposed to all of that. I'm not gonna lie, we were treading in what seemed like dangerous waters, but I knew I could trust Grandma Belle.

"Can we go see her?" Scott said. He was as anxious as I was to solve this Bulwark mystery. I looked at his face. He was so earnest. He had this cute dimple in his cheek. He brushed his hair away from his forehead, and said, "I am really happy we are doing this together."

Well, that did it. I had to ask. "What's up with your friend, Christopher?"

"Um… Chris. Yeah. We were close. I dunno." He shrugged.

"What do you mean, you were close?"

Scott fiddled with the zipper on his hoodie. "I… we were really tight when he first moved in. I mean, I like… liked him." Scott seemed to be struggling. "Look," he lowered his voice. "We're just not into the same things anymore. Don't get me wrong, he's still my friend…" He looked at me, his face draining of color. "You're not interested in him? He's kinda with Grace, you know, the head cheerleader."

I waved my hand in dismissal. "Me? Nah. That boy is not my type."

Scott sighed, almost like he was relieved or something. "That's a good thing," he said.

I looked at him then. The sun played with the golden highlights in his hair, and his eyes were watching me intently.

"Is it?" I asked softly. We didn't talk for a minute and then I said briskly, "Yeah, come on, let's go. I'm sure my Grandma would love a visit from her favorite grandchild, anyway." I replied. I hope Grandma Belle didn't mind me prying.

On the drive over to Grandma Belle's place, Scott reached over, one hand on the steering wheel, his other hand reached over onto mine.

"Don't worry, Sophia. I know we'll get this. We have to," Scott said to me. He was really concerned. I felt tingles, but I moved my hand away. I guess I was still rattled from Christopher, and I wondered how long that feeling would last. Anyway, we had to get answers, and fast. I looked at Scott and said, "I know. I'm not worried. Grandma Belle will know what to do."

When we arrived at my grandmother's house, she was sitting outside on her porch sipping a cup of tea. She set her cup down on the table next to her and sat up in her chair.

"Sophia? What are you doing here, baby? I wasn't expecting you," Grandma Bella said. She greeted me with a hug and kiss on the cheek. As she looked behind me she saw Scott. "And who is this?"

"Hi, Mrs.Beachwood," Scott said with a respectful wave.

"Grandma, this is Scott, my friend." I said.

"Nice to meet you." Scott went in to shake her hand.

"Oh, the pleasure is all mine, Scott." Grandma Belle shook his hand and gave me a wink. Her lips turned up at the ends with a grin and her eyes looked bright as if she knew something I didn't. Grandma Belle always showed a bit too much interest in my love life. She was gazing at Scott like I delivered her a juicy tidbit on a platter. I couldn't help but to roll my eyes.

"Grandma, we have some questions for you about your Cherokee heritage…" I was nervous to ask her. I fiddled with the notepad I held in my hands.

"Yes, Sophia. Come on, let's go inside. I'll make us a fresh pot of tea."

We followed her into her small ranch house as she guided us to the kitchen table. As Scott and I sat down, Grandma Belle ran a kettle of tea on the stove and sat down next to me.

She pulled down a metal tin filled with sugar cookies I knew she had baked. There was always homemade sugar cookies at her house. Every now and then, I caught her glancing our way. She cleared her throat and asked, "Sophia, is anything wrong?"

She knew me so well. I had the grace to blush. I stammered, "No. Not really."

Grandma raised an eyebrow and set a platter of cookies on the table.

"Now what is it, Sophia? I can see fear in your eyes."

My notepad was drenched with the sweat from my hands.

Scott said, "Give her the paper, Soph."

I pulled the limp paper from the last page of the notebook. I heard my grandmother gasp. I held it out with a shaking hand. She didn't take it at first.

The room was silent but for the ticking clock behind me on the wall. The silence was broken when the kettle screamed and we all jumped from our seats. I turned off the gas, but nobody moved to serve tea.

Scott and I laughed nervously, and Grandma Belle asked quietly, "Where did you get that?"

"A few nights ago on the football field we saw some people… I think… they were chanting." I said.

"Yes," Scott added. They kept repeating *bind them, free us.*"

"Go on," Grandma urged.

"As I approached them they vanished. I found this piece of paper left behind…"

Grandma Belle's eyes studied the paper. She rose wearily, to get mugs. Then she methodically poured the tea in each one and brought it to the table.

Both Scott and I sat straight in our seats, waiting for her to respond.

"Sophia, I've never shared things." She paused as if she was having trouble explaining. "Our ancestors lives are deeply connected to this town. As the village grows and changes, so do we have to adjust. We've lived here from the dawn of time. I never wanted to expose you to this until you were old enough to understand."

By this point I was jumping out of my skin. What the heck was she hiding from me and how was now the right time to expose family shit? I was mighty sorry Scott was sitting across from me and had no idea where she was going with this stuff.

She grabbed the paper in her fist. "This paper is part an ancient secret society of the Cherokee shamans. The people you saw on the field were a part of the secret sect. They come when they are needed, and right now they are needed. Was the field filled with a strange puddle?"

"Yes!" I exhaled. I hadn't realized I was holding my breath. "The grass was wet and smelled horrible, Grandma. I think that foul liquid has been seeping into our friend's lockers."

"This is bad news. Very bad." She shook her head and I swear, the hair on my arms stood straight up.

"Indeed," she continued. "The land was once praised by the shamans for it's sacred supply of water. Ever since the school was built upon that ground, the water supply diminished, eventually vanishing. This was very bad for our people. We got our strength, our power from that water. It's the source of life. The shamans are back. Not a good sign. They will want revenge."

"That's nuts! It sounds like a scary movie." I said.

"Sophia, no, I don't want you messing around with this. It's extremely dangerous. I don't think you understand…" Grandma Belle impaled me with her eyes. They had darkened like I have never seen them before. "This is no laughing matter, Sophie. They must do a sacrifice to appease the sacred water."

"Grandma, please. Our friends are being affected. Christopher and Chloe's lockers… there's been a strange smell and a heavy fog that comes out. Christopher can hear someone in his locker. We think it's the boy that went missing… Billy Joe Parker," I told her.

"Sophia, I said no!" Grandma Belle slapped her hand down on the table and gave me a furious look.

"What if it was me, Grandma? What if I was trapped? I can't just sit here." I was not giving up easily. Grandma Belle looked deep into my eyes for what felt like forever.

"Very well. I see the passion you hold. You must not be seen. A wrong move and you could be trapped like your friend."

"You mentioned the liquid as a bad sign... The school has been there for years. Why now?" Scott questioned.

"Have they done anything new?" Grandma Belle inquired.

Scott's voice sounded thin. "Astroturf on the football field. They got rid of the real grass."

"Ah ha. Mother earth cannot breath. She is choking. How could you breath if they covered you in plastic." Grandma Belle shook her head sadly.

"They will want revenge." Grandma Belle got up from her chair and walked toward her bookshelf. She took out an old, tattered book and flipped to a page toward the center.

"This passage." She pointed to the paper laying on the table. "It is only one of three parts to break the curse. The second part comes from this book." She held up an ancient book, the cover stained.

"This is the Book of Shadows. If the shamans were chanting *bind them, free us* they are banishing someone from our world and sending them to another. For one to be free, another must be enslaved. The only way to break the curse is to go to the banishing portal and retrieve the other half of the spell. It's most likely hidden within the portal, which means you'll have to enter in order to find it."

"Enter a portal? I don't know... How are we even supposed to know where this portal is?" I asked.

"If you look closely, you will find it. See here?" Grandma Belle pointed to the symbol on the paper I brought. "Look for the double horns of salvation. They will protect you... Here, take this." Grandma Belle ripped out the page in her Book of Shadows.

"You'll need this. But listen to me closely. Your answer lies in the shadow of death. Do not be afraid, Sophia. Any sniff of fear will alert the dogs. You must find the final part to the curse within the portal. Without it, you won't be able to get out."

The passage read,
"By shackles we were bound
by earth and sacred ground
We freed thy strains
And locked the liberated in chains"

"Locked the liberated in chains?" Scott looked at me like he had just seen a ghost. I shook my head and went on.

"Where is the entrance?" I asked.

"It's where you hear the victims calling. This is your destiny, Sophia. You alone must go."

"But Grandma…"

"Fate has connected you to the curse, it runs in your blood and though you cannot fight this savage civilization, you must protect the innocent."

"You speak as if you know more," Scott said quietly.

Grandma Belle nodded. "I made this trip when they build the school on the land. It's hard for me to remember everything from back then. Most of it is a blank. It was a dangerous journey, but well worth it. I rescued the boy who became your grandfather."

"I'm not marrying Billy Joe!" I said with passion.

Grandma laughed. "You are a brave girl. " She looked at Scott. "No, your future lies elsewhere, but this is a job you must do."

I embraced my grandmother and detected her tremble with fear. This did not fill me with a lot of confidence, but I knew I had no choice.

All I kept thinking about is this portal. How am I going to pull this off? I'm just a high school student. This was going to take every ounce of bravery I had left.

Scott drove me home. He didn't hold my hand this time. We were both in our own thoughts a bit.

"I'll do it," Scott said to me.

I was silent for a moment. My grandmother said I had to do it. I shook my head. "No Scott. We both know it has to be me."

What if we didn't find the portal? And moreover, what if we didn't find the last part of the curse? I could be locked in this portal forever. My mind was going a million miles per second. When we pulled up to my house and the car stopped my mind was so filled with thoughts I didn't move to leave. We sat in silence for a bit and I finally turned to Scott.

"We'll let Chloe and Christopher know what we found out and devise a plan tomorrow night. We'll all meet at the school to finish this," I said.

"Tomorrow night it is. Good night, Sophia."

I nodded and went inside. I stood by the door watching Scott. He stayed a long time looking at my door. At last, he drove away.

12

Dear Diary

I haven't had a chance to write for a few days. I've been so mixed up. I had to process the rest of the events of that fateful evening. The night that changed my life forever. I will never take my freedom for granted again. Let me do my best to recount the night as well as I can.

Scott, Chloe, Christopher and I went back to the school as we planned. It was about eleven-thirty, way past curfew. We all had to sneak past our parents and out of our houses this time. It was risky. If we got caught, we could all be expelled. Or worse, Sheriff Finnes could arrest us.

All four of us were tense with worry. I could tell nobody had slept the night before.

"Let's hurry up. The later I'm out, the worse trouble I'll get from my parents.

Hopefully they don't notice I'm gone."
Christopher said.

I wanted to mention he didn't seem as
nervous when he met up with Grace Kelly on
the sly. We went straight to the locker again.
The hallways were deserted, filled with a
ghostly silence. The air was chilled and
goosebumps ran down my spine. This time as
we approached Christopher's locker, it slowly
creaked open on its own.

"Woah… it's like it knows we're
here…" Scott said, jumping back in surprise.
We crept closer to it and heard the voice of
Billy Joe. A suppressed yell echoed, "Free
me!"

Christopher's eyes widened. "That's
just like what those people were chanting the
other night… "Free us…"

"Yeah, um, those people, Chris, we're
a secret cult…" Scott blurted out.

"Huh?" Christopher looked stunned.

"Yeah, that's how we looked when we
found out, too," Scott replied.

"My grandma knew about the
shaman's secret society, so Scott and I asked
her a few questions. She told us the paper we
found is part of a curse. The second part my
grandma gave to use out of her Book of
Shadows."

" This sounds stupid. How do I know
you're telling the truth?" Christopher said
suspiciously.

"Shut up, Chris. She's telling the truth," Scott said.

I continued, "In order to break the curse, we need to find a portal and recover the final part of this spell. My grandma said that on the other side of the portal is a place where there's constraint. The shamans cast this spell on the students because the land's been desecrated."

"Why the students? They should go after the teachers!" Christopher said.

"Or at least the administration." Chloe replied.

Scott shrugged and said "Suffer the children?"

Wow, I didn't realize how smart Scott was. I responded, "Sure… nobody would care if grown-ups were disappearing, but they *do* care about missing kids."

We heard a scuffle around the corner. All four of us turned to see the janitor, Trout Parker rushing toward us. There was a shotgun in his hand.

"He's got a gun!" Scott yelled. He grabbed me and we raced down the hall.

"Stop," he screamed. It came out like a sob. I slowed. Trout Parker was crying. "I won't hurt you. Let me explain," he called breathlessly.

We stopped, our hearts racing. Trout skidded to a halt. He called out, "Principal Heart lets me stay overnight to guard the school. It's the only way I can stay close to my nephew, Billy Joe. He's trapped in there," Trout puffed, out of breath, pointing to the locker.

We heard a muffled yell come from the locker.

"That's it, I'm going in. Stand back!" I nervously said. I reached inside the locker and felt nothing. Not a back wall, or metal sides. I reached deeper, my hand grew cold.

"What's inside, Sophia?" I heard Scott say, but a mist surrounded me.

I leaned forward. I felt drawn to the darkness and fell. Diary, I don't know what it was, but a force pulled me in. Everything went black. All I could hear is the howling of wind and what sounded like a thousand voices crying out. A lash of a whip sounded in the distance and light peered through the bottom of a door.

"Where am I?" I said. I landed on a dusty floor. Light seeped in through warped wooden walls. Dust motes danced around me.

I stood carefully and went over to the door to peer through a knothole.

There he was. Billy Joe. He was standing outside. I opened the door, yanked Billy Joe inside, and slammed it shut.

"Billy Joe," I whispered urgently.

He spun. "Sophia Beachwood? How... how did you get here?" Billy Joe looked like his uncle Trout, with his mouth working.

"We heard you through Christopher's locker. Never mind that, what is this place?" I asked.

"Keep it down. I don't want the others to hear you… I've been here for what seems like forever. Time moves differently in this place. Slower. We're stuck in another time," Billy Joe whispered.

"What?" I peered outside..

"No stop!" He stood in front of the door. "You can't go out there. They are gonna grab you."

I must have looked puzzled.

"It's 1862. You really shouldn't be here. We have to get out before they see you. Don't you understand?"

He touched my arm. "Your skin color… If they see you, they're gonna capture you and make you a slave. You don't have papers. They are gonna say you're a runaway. Can you get us outta here?"

Just then I heard yelling from the other side of the door.

"Billy Joe, where'd you go? You talkin' to yourself again? I hear you."

The voices past the door, becoming fainter. I waited until I couldn't hear anything and peeked outside. Billy Joe pulled me back, but i surged outside. I whispered to him urgently, "If you want to get out of here I have to find the twin horns."

I ran. I got a stitch in my side. I had no idea where I was running. I leaped into the brush. Branches tore at my clothes, scratched my face. I felt winded, but I didn't stop. Dogs barked, and their noise was drown by my own gulping breath. I found a hiding spot behind a tree, paused and picked up a blade of grass. It reminded of home. I tucked it away in my bra where I kept the two curses for safe keeping. Hands grabbed me. "What she wearin'? I heard someone yell. "Britches. Where'd you steal these from, girl?" A bag was placed over my head and I my arms were pulled backward in a vice like grip. I felt like my shoulders were being torn from their sockets. I wondered how my grandmother failed to mention this might happen. I started to scream.

I heard a man say, "What in tarnation? She is wearin' pants?"

I was punched hard in the shoulder. "Hush up, child, or you'll be sorry!"

"Where are you taking me?" I shouted.

Something hard hit my skull and I was knocked out cold.

When I awoke I had shackles around my hands and feet. They were connected by heavy iron chains. The air was heavy with the odor of manure. I gagged from the smell.

I was on a dirt floor in a barn. My head hurt. I looked around and saw others tied up as well.

"What's going on? Where are we?" I said groggily.

"Child, we're being sold today. It's New Year's Day, auction day. Get to meet our new master. I hear Mr. Bern's is good to his slaves."

"Slaves? Who are you?"

"They call me Andrew, but you can call me Andy."

I looked around. My eyes were still blurry from the blow to my head "Where's Billy Joe?"

"He's with Mr. Berns. Mr. Berns took a liking to that boy." He shook his head. "I don't know why, but he likes him."

I looked around to see if anyone was watching us. I took out the blade of grass I had placed away, pursed my lips together and blew on the strand of grass. I wished for Scott, Chloe or Christopher to hear me like they heard Billy through the locker. I didn't get too far. Someone heard me, alright, but it wasn't who I hoped. We heard noise coming from outside the door. Two men came in. One man said, "Get up. They're waitin' on you now, go!"

We were lead out to an auction block. There was Billy Joe again. He moved his head with a slight nod. We couldn't talk to each other in that moment, but we knew we both had to help each other out. When it came to my turn to be on the market, I saw Billy Joe whisper to slave owner Mr. Berns.

"Sold!" Was this real? I'm a slave and I was just sold? WTF! I looked at the cold hard stares of the people surrounding me. They were selling humans. They were lined up like cattle. We were nothing more than property. One man approached me with a whip. He pushed the handle of the whip under my chin.

"This one's full of vinegar. She gonna be a handful." I felt fury build in my chest. I forced myself to calm. We were lead away, our chains rubbing our skin raw. The pain was excruciating.

They backed us against the side of the barn.

Billy Joe approached me. He was not having any trouble walking around. Nobody seemed to even notice him.

"This is a good thing, Bern's buying you. This way we'll be together." Billy Joe said.

"Billy Joe, I can't be here. We can't be here. Have you seen anything like this?"

I showed Billy Joe the first curse we found and point to the symbol on it. "It's called the double horns of salvation. I have two parts of a curse to get us out of here. Will you help me find the final piece?"

I heard the crack of a whip snap in the hot air. "Get moving!" It was Mr. Berns' men gathering us up. "Time to go."

We all piled into a cart. The ride was long and dusty. I choked on the thick air. Soon I was covered with dirt. When we arrived at the house, I could see slaves picking the cotton in the fields surround the mansion. I was dragged toward a small rickety cabin. Inside a row of females were handing out clothes. I changed quickly and came outside. I saw Billy Joe and a few other men deep in the fields overseeing the workers. I made eye contact with Billy Joe and put his finger to his mouth.

"I have to go back to town for Mr. Berns. He told me to take a female. Give me that one" Billy Joe pointed to me as he was sitting on top of a cart. "You. Come with me, girl."

One of the overseers made a lurid comment. I felt the skin tighten on my scalp and I had to fight the urge to punch him. Instead a scurried over to the wagon and hauled myself into the rear.

No one seemed to question Billy Joe's propriety air.

I scrambled toward the front of the wagon and asked, "How come you can do that?"

"The dogs. I helped Mr. Berns with one of his dogs."

I knew the Parkers kept a kennel of wild looking dogs back in our time. I nodded. It made sense." They don't know shit about taking care of dogs here. I fixed one of his bitches and since then I can't do nuthin' wrong."

"You sound almost as though you like it here."

"Well," he said. "Strange as it seems back home I don't get no respect. Here, they think I'm pretty smart."

"Still," I said bitterly, looking at the people sweating in the fields.

"I know, I know. Slavery is horrible. Don't get me wrong, I want to go home."

It was quiet. No planes, trains or cars. The air was different too, sweeter. The sun burned on my face. My hair was pulled up in a turban, but the heat bore into me.

We drove for what seemed like an hour. "Where we going?" I called out.

"Shush!" he yelled back. I knew he was being cautious, but being told what to do rankled.

We pulled into a small churchyard, the tombstones were crooked in the cemetery.

Billy Joe stopped the horses, leaped down and pointed to two church steeples.

"Been thinkin' a bit. You think those look like the twin horns you've been talkin' 'bout.? I can't think of nuthin' else except steer. Come on," he called as he walked to the church door. The door swung open, Scott stood on the other side.

"What are you doing here?" I was relieved. I fought the urge to run over and hug him.

"Your grass trick worked! I heard your call and I went in the locker after you. I've been following you ever since, keeping a low profile." Scott explained. I didn't even think. I fell into his arms and hugged him. I felt his arms wrap around me and hold me tight.

"What now?" Billy Joe asked. "We better get going soon, before they figure out I didn't go to town."

I pulled out the two spells from inside my shirt.

"Let's find the last curse!" Scott said.

"I'm not sure about this place. How do we know we've got the right twin horns?" I asked.

"Didn't you see the name of the church? Sheppard's Salvation. You said look for the double horns of salvation. That's what lead me here" Scott said.

I spun in a small circle and shrugged. "I don't know where to look for the third paper."

"Think Sophia. There has to be something..."

My mind raced over the words. In the distance we could hear the sound of Mr. Bern's dogs barking.

"They're looking for us. We have to hurry," Billy Joe said urgently.

I stumbled to the nearest pew. The dogs sounded like they were getting closer. Fear made me immobile.

"Here.. look. This here is how I was able to see you." Billy Joe pointed to a framed oval mirror in the back of the church.

"Sophie!" Scott snapped me out of my stupor. "It's here. The portal."

We skittered up the aisle to stare into the mirror. I looked in and I could see Chloe and Christopher. Chloe was taking more pictures with her phone while Christopher was absorbed in his cellphone.

"Help." I cried. Billy Joe smothered my call by putting his hand over my mouth.

"Are you crazy? Do you want to get caught again? We can't be seen or heard in here." Billy Joe looked at me sternly. I nodded and he let his hand down.

"Where do you think the last curse could be found?" Scott asked.

"Do you remember anything else your Grandma said, Sophia? Any ideas?" Scott asked.

"I don't know, Scott. You were there too, Scott… wait. She did say the answers are

in shadow of death… what could that mean?"
I said.

I surveyed the room. All I saw was a
sea of Bibles. The perfect place to hide a piece
of paper.

"The bibles. Let's search them." I
said. We scrambled to the pews and began
opening bibles, leafing through the pages.

"Psalm 23! "Yea, though I walk
through the valley of the shadow of death,"…
you guys! The answer is in one of these
Bibles! Look for the page with Psalm 23 on
it!" Scott said.

We scanned through every Bible for
Psalm 23. It felt like we were trying to find a
needle in a haystack. There were so many
Bibles. I grabbed a black Bible. It was
different than the rest. The other Bibles were
blue. It was heavier, and the pages were
yellowed and mottled. I leafed through it,
page after page, searching for the Psalm. The
dogs were barking madly.

"Hurry!" Scott urged.
The next page I turned over was Psalm 23. A
loose paper fell out.
"Psalm 23… this is it!" There it was… the final
curse to reverse the original one.
"Here, the third piece" I said.

Scott recited the first curse, Billy Joe
the second. I read the third,
"By the elements of earth and water

*By the journey traveled by our sons and
daughters
Accelerate the hands of time back to
perfection
And soon you will see through your own
reflection"*

We each read the spells allowed one
by one. The mirror glass started to ripple as if
it was water. I touched it with my fingertip
and my hand slipped through.

The church doors burst open. Six men
with a pack of howling dogs filled the church.
Scott pushed me through the mirror. I fell
into nothingness, my head swimming. I called
for Scott, hoping he made it out. I could see
nothing.

I landed, tumbling out of the locker.
Billy Joe plopped down next to me.

"Scott!" I screamed scrambling to my
feet. "Scott!"

He appeared out of thin air, falling
against me. Scott got up and slammed the
locker door shut. A deafening silence fell over
us. The portal was closed. We clung to each
other, laughing. A swell of emotions came
rushing over me and I leaned into him. He
kissed me, our lips pressed tightly against each
other. Diary, it was everything I've ever hoped
for.

"What are you wearing?" Chloe asked.
"Are you okay?"

"Dude!" Christopher slapped Billy Joe in the back. "I knew you were in there. I'm gonna request a locker change, just to be safe…" Christopher said looking deeply into the locker's interior.

"Billy Joe, what happened?"

Trout Parker grabbed his nephew. "Man, you gave us a scare."

"You don't know the half of it," Billy Joe told his uncle. "I just want to go home right now and see my dogs."

"Yeah, let's get you home, boy!"

We all walked out the doors of the school.

"Do you think it's over?" Scott said

"One way to tell," I said.

We walked out to the field. The grass felt different. I knelt down. The AstroTurf was gone. In its place was new grass. "Hey, " I yelled to Trout Parker. "What happened to the fake grass?"

"Oh, Principal Heart removed it last night. Said it was creating some mold problem."

I looked up at the full moon. Across the field a hooded figure was walking. It turned. The bright moon illuminated the face of the man. He nodded once and disappeared into the darkness.

Scott put his arms around me. I felt safe. I felt at home. I was happy.

13

OCTOBER 31ST

Dear Diary,

Well, we made it to Halloween. All my friends are out and about, except for me. Even Christopher. He's on a date with Grace Kelly. I think they are dressed like Frankenstein and his wife.

I'm home eating popcorn, with Scott and Chloe watching Mary Poppins, the first one, not the scary one. You know, with Julie Andrews. A Spoonful of Sugar is about all I can handle right now. After Billy Joe came home, there was a welcome home party and the mayor lifted the town curfew.

I can't dress up. I can't pretend to be afraid. The costume are so… silly. The kids, they don't understand real fear. It's not funny or fun. No. Real fear stays forever.

My story. It never made the papers. In the end, nobody would believe me. I don't care, I'm not going to let that stop me. I may have quit cheerleading, but I won't stop fighting for the truth. Right now, Scott and I want to do more research. We are going to apply to the same school.

We want to understand what really happened in Bulwark and the only way this cat can find out is to keep digging. Hopefully, the curiosity won't kill me. Until then, meow!

AUTHOR'S NOTE

I wrote The Darkness out of inspiration by author Brit Lunden. She is brilliantly creative and a role model to all. Thank you for your support and guidance. To R.L. Jackson, your passion and originative ideas are outstanding and beautiful. I'd like to give a personal thank you to all of my friends and family. It's been a long, crazy road together. I wouldn't change it for the world. This one is for the women in my family. We went through the darkness and made it out stronger than ever.

In The Darkness, Sophia is searching for her "Prince Charming" before the madness ensues. I dedicate this book to my one true love. Franklyn, thank you for being my everything. When life gets hard you're there to cushion the struggle. I was meant to walk this earth with you. Thank you for your unconditional love and reinforcement. Thank you for always seeing me for me. I love you over the moon, across the stars and back… always and forever.

For more on my books or to get in touch with
me–

Like my Facebook page-
facebook.com/brittneybass

Follow me on Twitter-
twitter.com/BrittneyBass

Huge thanks to cover designer R.L. Jackson
authorrljackson.com

Read the rest of the Bulwark Anthology!

Bulwark by Brit Lunden

The Knowing, Volume 1 by Brit Lunden

The Illusion, Volume 2 by DJ Cooper

The Craving, Volume 3 by R.L. Jackson

The Window, Volume 4 by E.H. Graham

The Missing Branch, Volume 5 by Kay MacLeod

The Body, Volume 6 by Kate Kelley

The Battle of Bulwark, Volume 7 by Del Henderson III

The Darkness, Volume 8 by Brittney Leigh

If you enjoyed this story, please leave a review on Amazon, Goodreads, or wherever else you love to talk about books. Thank you!

CPSIA information can be obtained
at www.ICGtesting.com
Printed in the USA
FFHW021953210319
51158286-56651FF

9 781950 080007